⬛MOJANG
MINECRAFT

EGMONT

We bring stories to life

First published in Great Britain 2016 as Exploded Builds: Medieval Fortress
by Egmont UK Limited, The Yellow Building,
1 Nicholas Road, London W11 4AN
This edition published in 2018

Written by Craig Jelley
Designed by Joe Bolder, Ryan Marsh and Martin Johansson/Mojang AB.
Illustrations by Joe Bolder and Ryan Marsh.
Production by Christine Campbell.
Special thanks to Lydia Winters, Owen Jones, Markus Toivonen,
Martin Johansson, Marsh Davies and Jesper Öqvist.

A big thank you to all of our testers: Adam Rayment, Alex Gibberd, Alexander Parker,
Bailey Whitehead Browne, Cormac Gilmore, Daniel Scott Phillips, Eden Kneale, Emma Verghese,
Ethan Wilson, Fred Fox, Grace Noble, Isaac Riordan, Jack Dillon, Jack Moody, Jackson Givens,
Jane Simmons, Joseph Sneddon, Marco Kahlhamer, Miranda Ryan-White, Molly Ellerbeck,
Noah Killeen, Oliver Berridge, Oscar Riordan, Robert Simmons, Sami Fyfe, Skye Ingram,
Theo Smith, Thomas Dillon, Thomas Hone, Wilfred Weston.

© 2018 Mojang AB and Mojang Synergies AB. MINECRAFT is a trademark or registered trademark
of Mojang Synergies AB.

All rights reserved.

MOJANG

ISBN 978 1 4052 9192 7
68856/001
Printed in China

ONLINE SAFETY FOR YOUNGER FANS

Spending time online is great fun! Here are a few simple rules to help younger fans stay safe and keep the
internet a great place to spend time:

- Never give out your real name – don't use it as your username.
- Never give out any of your personal details.
- Never tell anybody which school you go to or how old you are.
- Never tell anybody your password except a parent or a guardian.
- Be aware that you must be 13 or over to create an account on many sites. Always check the site policy and
ask a parent or guardian for permission before registering.
- Always tell a parent or guardian if something is worrying you.

Stay safe online. Any website addresses listed in this book are correct at the time of going to print.
However, Egmont is not responsible for content hosted by third parties. Please be aware that online
content can be subject to change and websites can contain content that is unsuitable for children. We
advise that all children are supervised when using the internet.

The publishers have used every endeavour to trace copyright owners and secure appropriate
permissions for materials reproduced in this book. In case of any unintentional omission,
the publishers will be pleased to hear from the relevant copyright owner.

Egmont takes its responsibility to the planet and its inhabitants very seriously. All the papers we use are from well-
managed forests run by responsible suppliers.

MOJANG
MINECRAFT
MEDIEVAL CASTLE

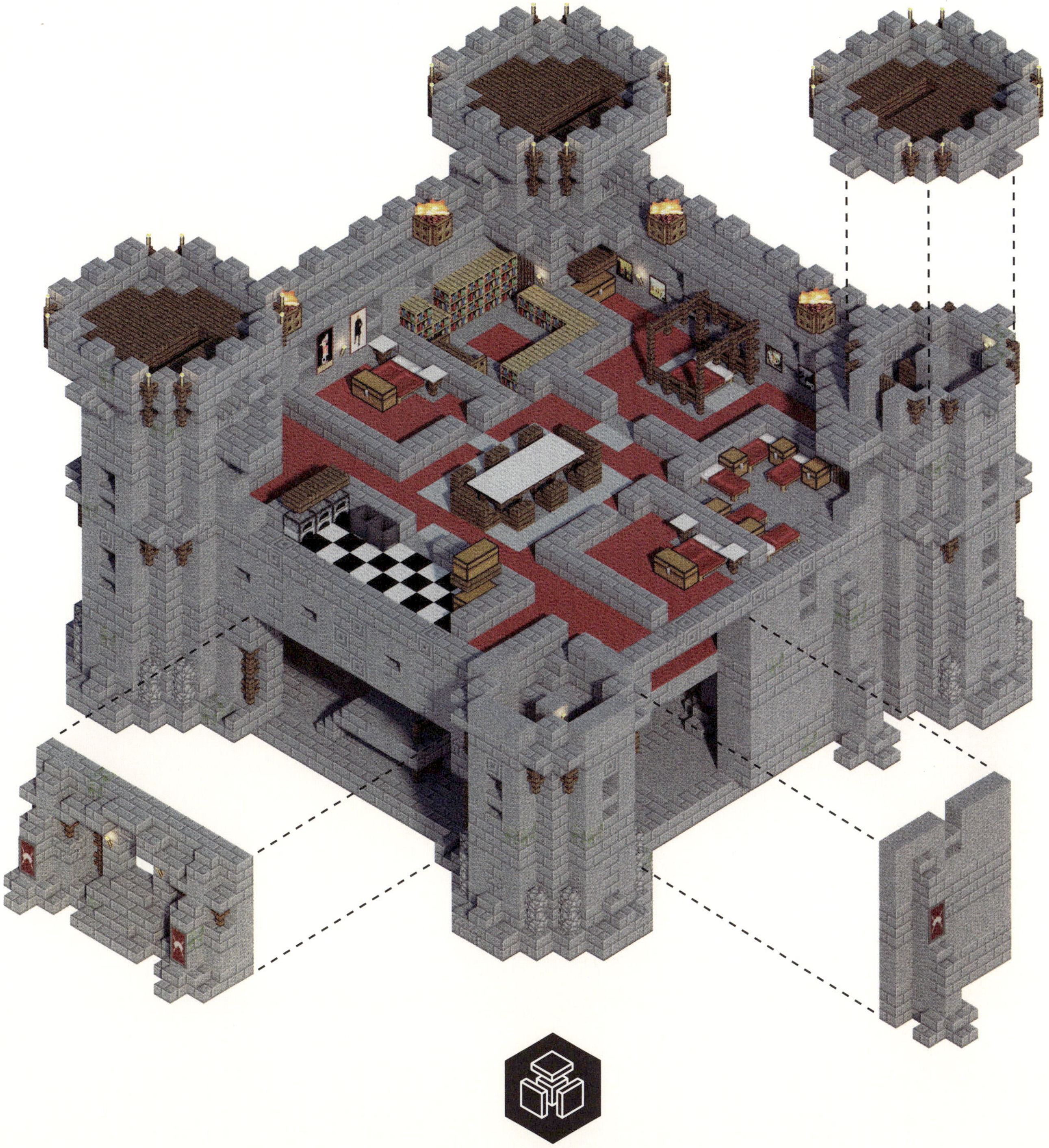

EXPLODED
BUILDS

CONTENTS

Turret ------------------------------- ◆ 6

Outer Wall ---------------------------- ◆ 8

Castle Keep --------------------------- ◆ 10

Throne Room -------------------------- ◆ 12

Barracks ----------------------------- ◆ 14

Enchanting Room ---------------------- ◆ 16

Dungeon ------------------------------ ◆ 18

Village House ------------------------- ◆ 20

Market Square ------------------------ ◆ 22

Finishing Touches --------------------- ◆ 24

KINGDOM LAYOUT

The layout of your kingdom is almost as important as the buildings in it. Below is a map of an example kingdom to use as a guide, with page references for each of the builds. Build your castle on high ground to give you an advantage over attackers.

Inside the Castle Keep

12
16
18

TURRET

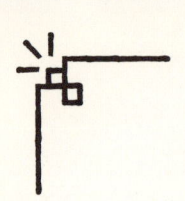

⏱ 0.5 HOURS ❶ ❷ ❸ ❹ BEGINNER

To keep creepers, zombies and marauding enemies away from your castle, you'll need to see them coming. The first blocks you place in your fortress will become the turrets – made from brick blocks, they will allow you to watch over a wider area, and see enemies in the distance. Add turrets where two walls meet at the corners of your fortress, so you can view the whole kingdom.

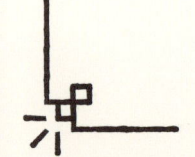

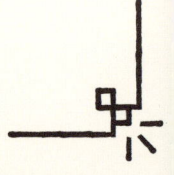

Turrets were types of towers that extended above the castle walls, or were built on top of other, larger towers.

Turrets and other castle structures had arrow loops – small, thin openings that allowed archers to shoot at attackers whilst remaining mostly protected.

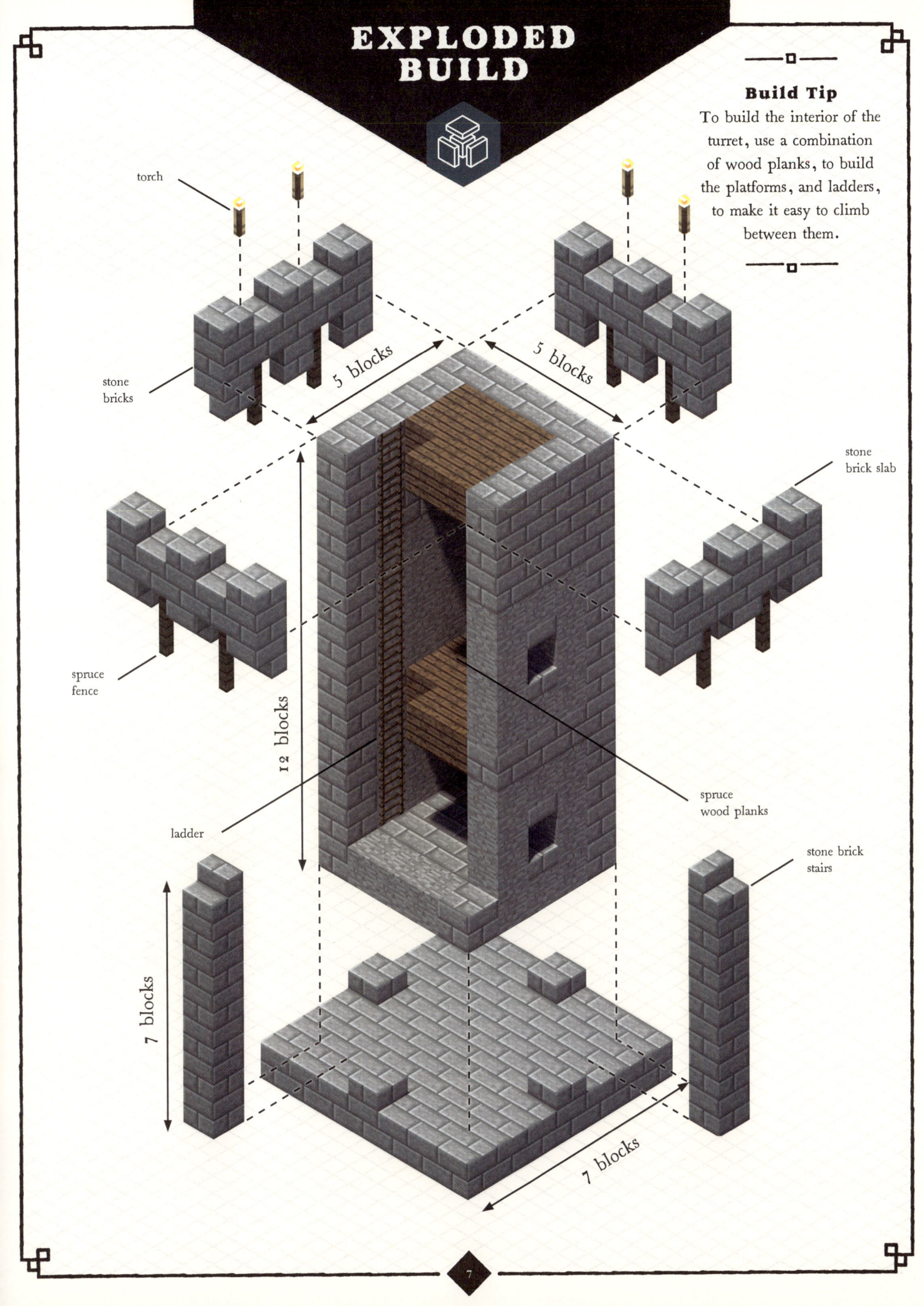

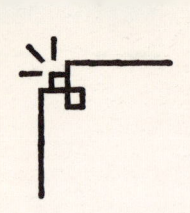

OUTER WALL

⏱ 1.5 HOURS ① ② ③ ④ EASY

Now you've got the turrets in place, it's time to build the fortifications. Every structure you build will be within this outer wall, so make sure that it's large enough. The wall will be your first line of defence against outsiders, so it needs to be made from durable blocks. You might need to destroy part of the wall to build turrets later on, but the most important thing is to get the size and shape of your fortress correct.

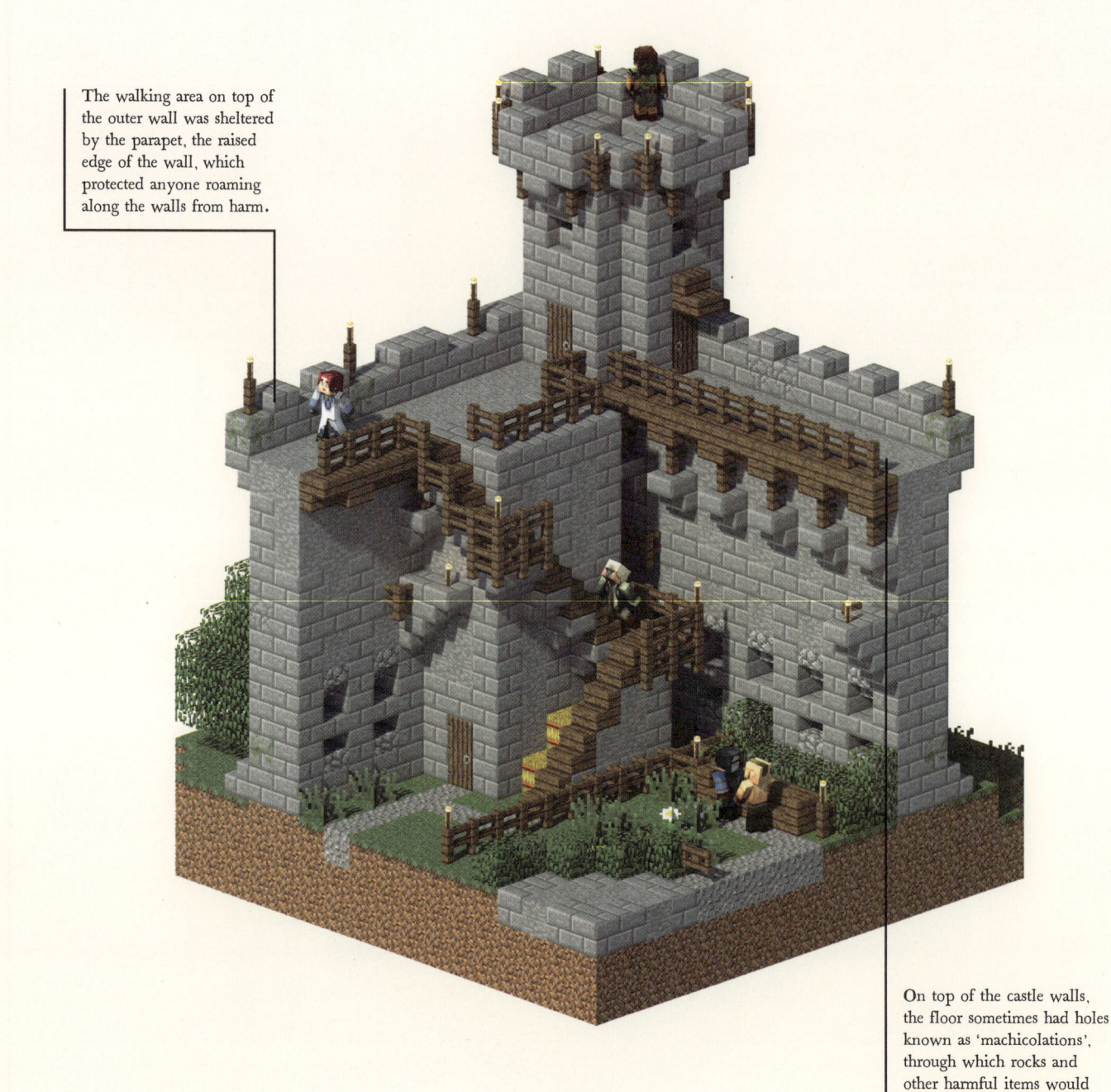

The walking area on top of the outer wall was sheltered by the parapet, the raised edge of the wall, which protected anyone roaming along the walls from harm.

On top of the castle walls, the floor sometimes had holes known as 'machicolations', through which rocks and other harmful items would be dropped on attackers.

8

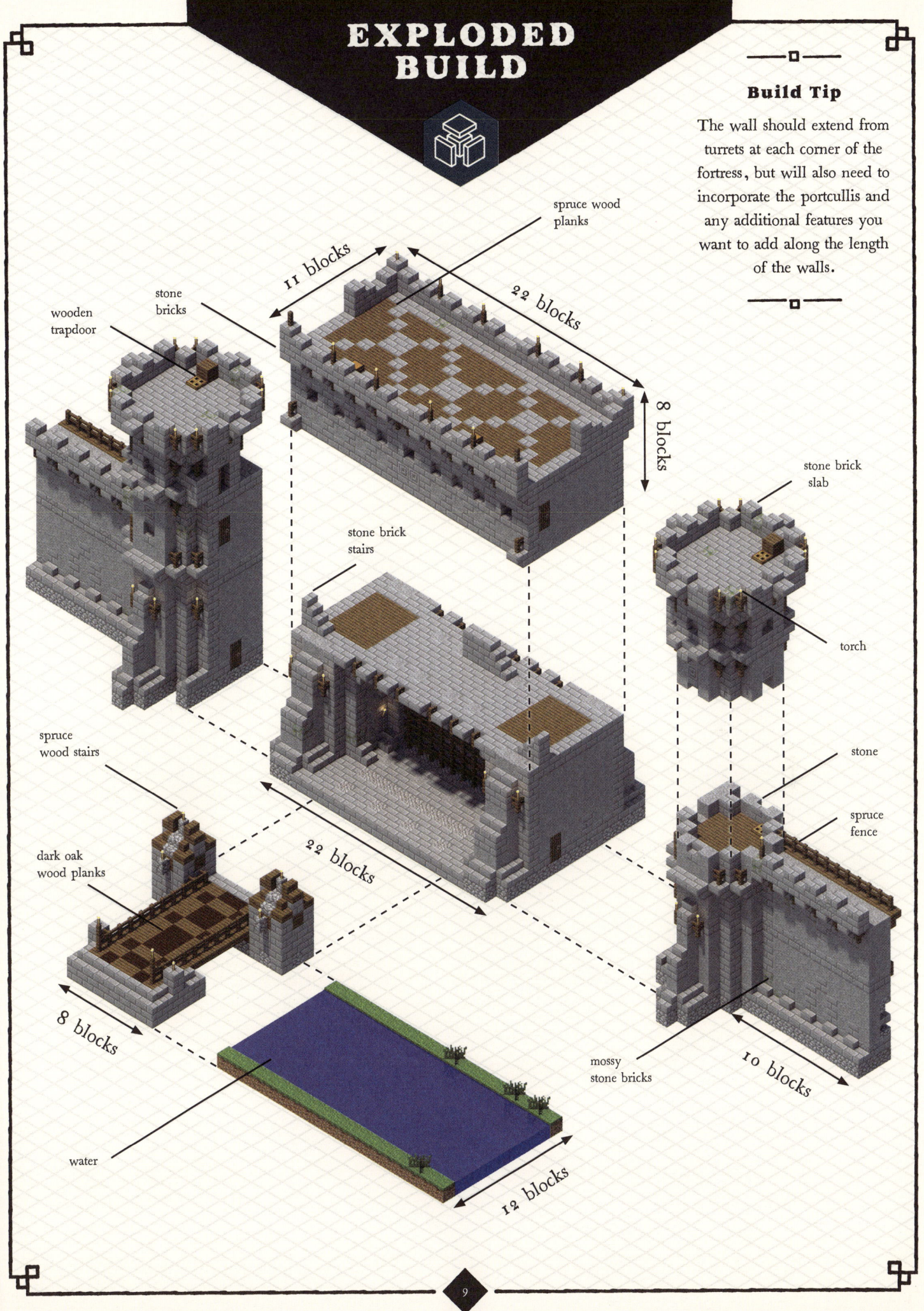

CASTLE KEEP

⏱ 4 HOURS ① ② ③ ④ INTERMEDIATE

Now it's time to build the centrepiece of your fortress – the castle itself. This will be your home as the ruler of the fortress and the citadel within it. The castle will feature the room builds in the following sections and can be used to house the rest of your medieval clan.

The battlement was the walking area atop the castle. It could cover the entire area, or just the perimeter.

Castles often had putlog – or sometimes 'putlock' – holes, which were used to provide support to temporary structures or scaffolds.

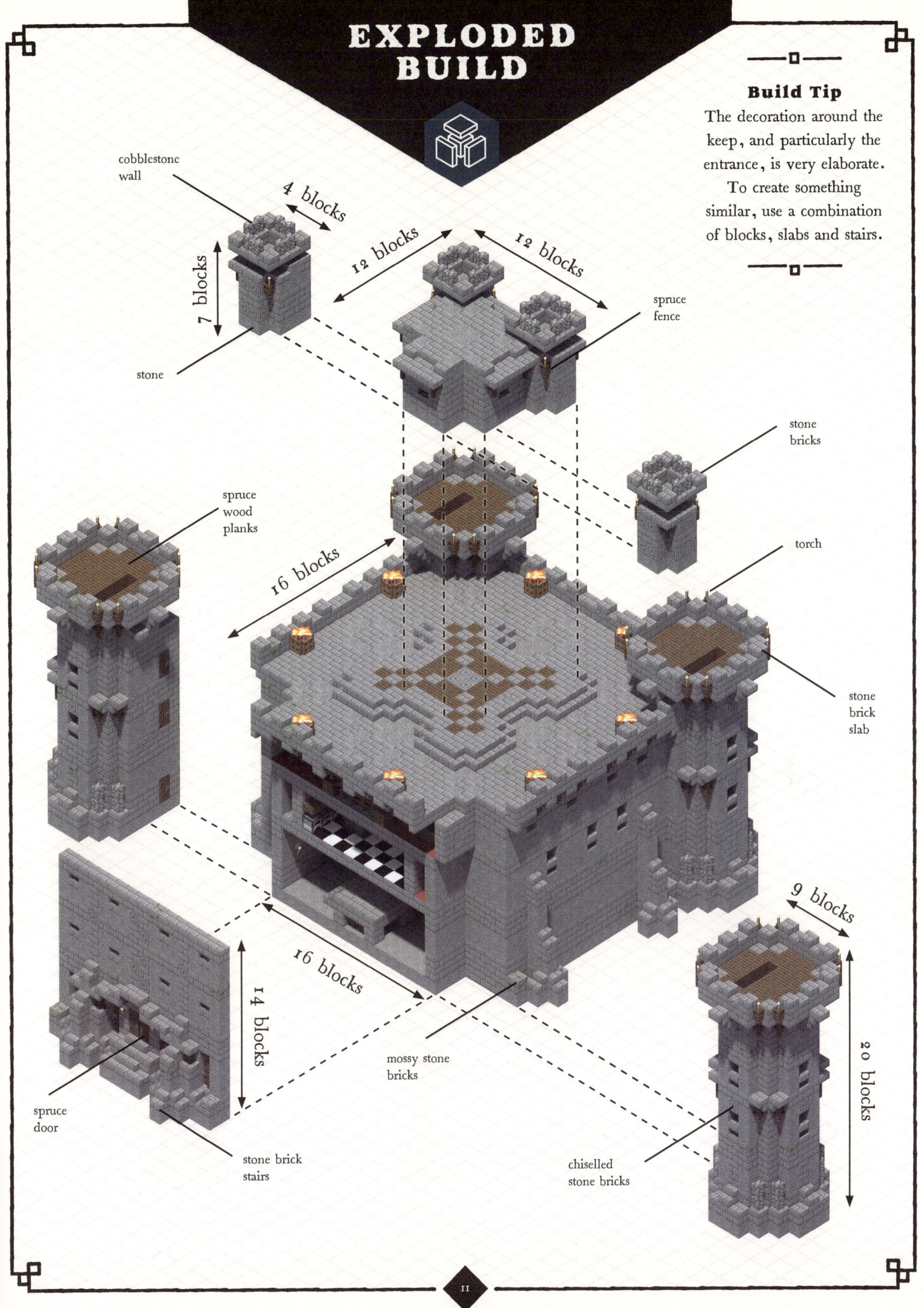

THRONE ROOM

⏲ 0.5 HOURS ⬢1 ②③④ BEGINNER

Every good king or queen needs a throne room from which to rule over their stronghold and this one should be no different. Whether there are raids on an ore-rich cave to plan, or preparations needed to fend off the latest wave of invaders, the throne room is the perfect place to conduct official business.

Medieval monarchies would often have two thrones together, one for a king, the other for the queen.

The thrones were often situated on plinths to raise the rulers above everyone else in the room.

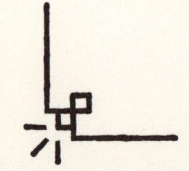

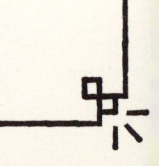

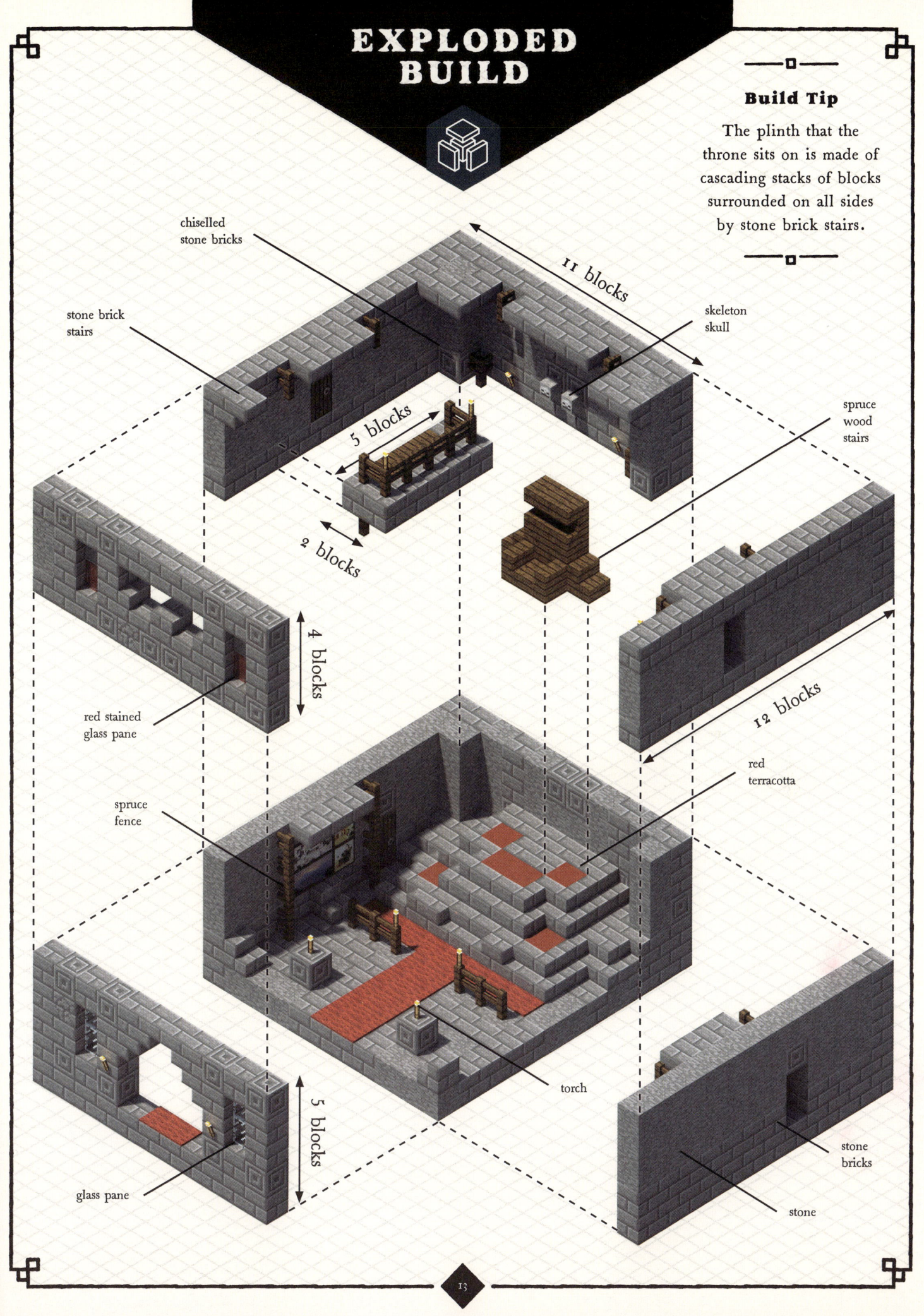

BARRACKS

🕐 1 HOUR ① ② ③ ④ EASY

With a huge clan following you, you'll need to make sure they can survive the world outside of the castle walls. The barracks is the best place to train with your friends and store armour and weapons, so you can easily fend off encroaching spiders, zombies and invaders.

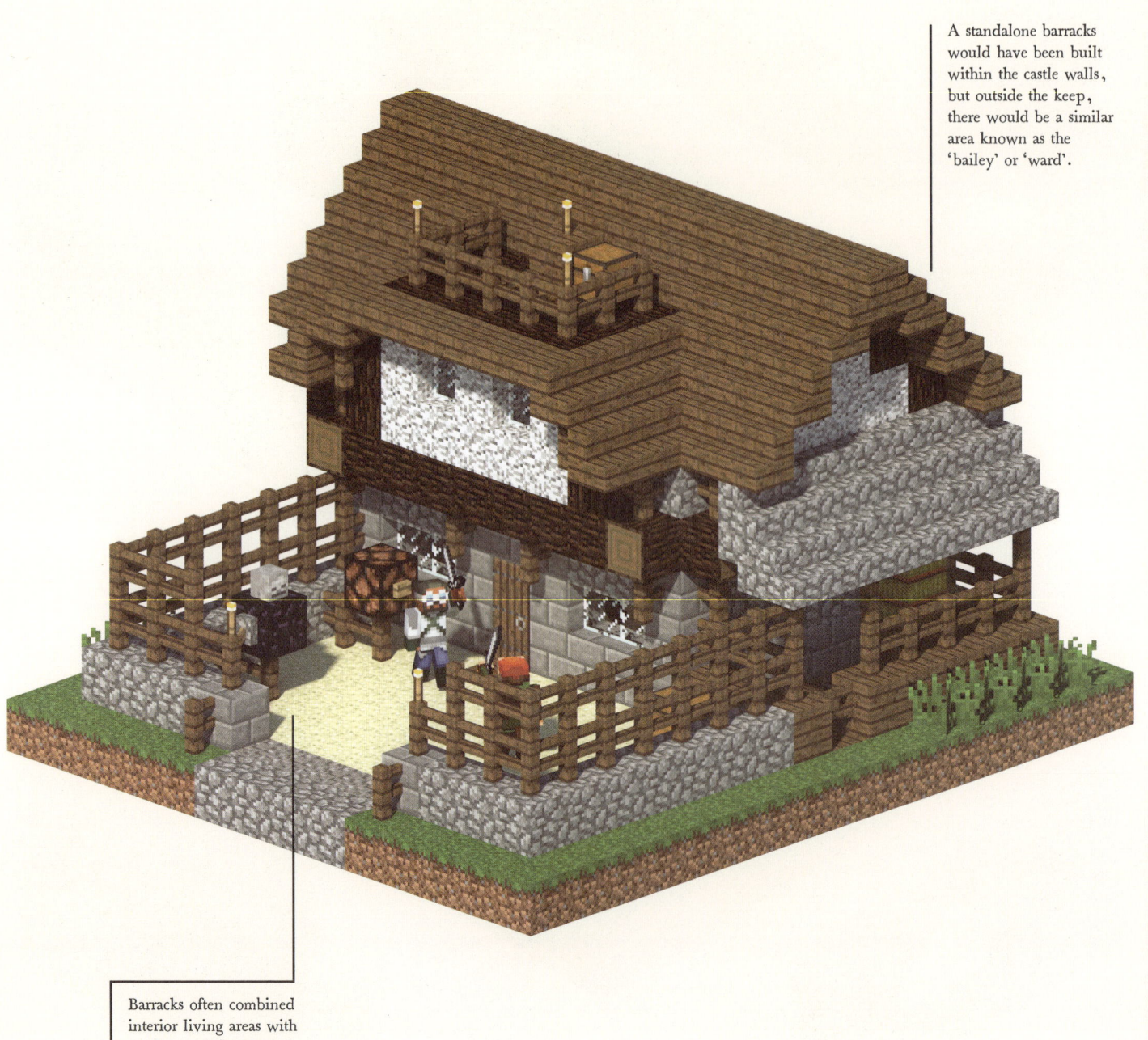

A standalone barracks would have been built within the castle walls, but outside the keep, there would be a similar area known as the 'bailey' or 'ward'.

Barracks often combined interior living areas with outdoor practice spaces.

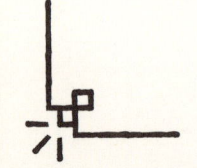

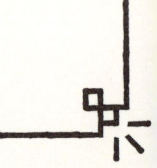

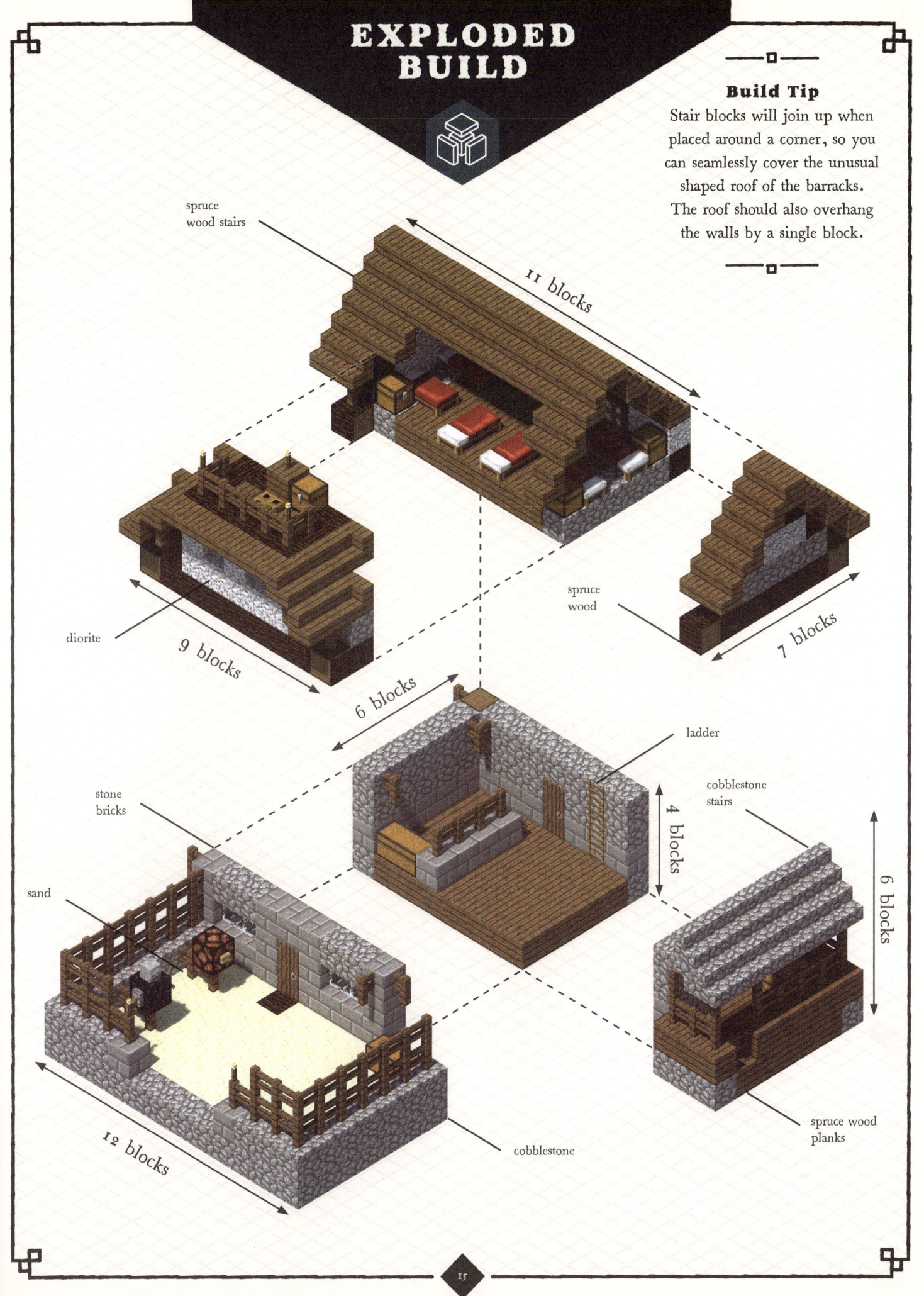

EXPLODED BUILD

Build Tip
Stair blocks will join up when placed around a corner, so you can seamlessly cover the unusual shaped roof of the barracks. The roof should also overhang the walls by a single block.

ENCHANTING ROOM

🕐 1 HOUR   ❶ ❷ ❸ ❹   EASY

If attackers are starting to cause you problems and are on the verge of breaching your stronghold's defences, a bit of magic might be just the thing you need to turn the battle around. Send your best mages and wizards to the enchanting room to cook up potions to buff your clan – or weaken the invaders – and create special arrows that could tip the balance in your favour.

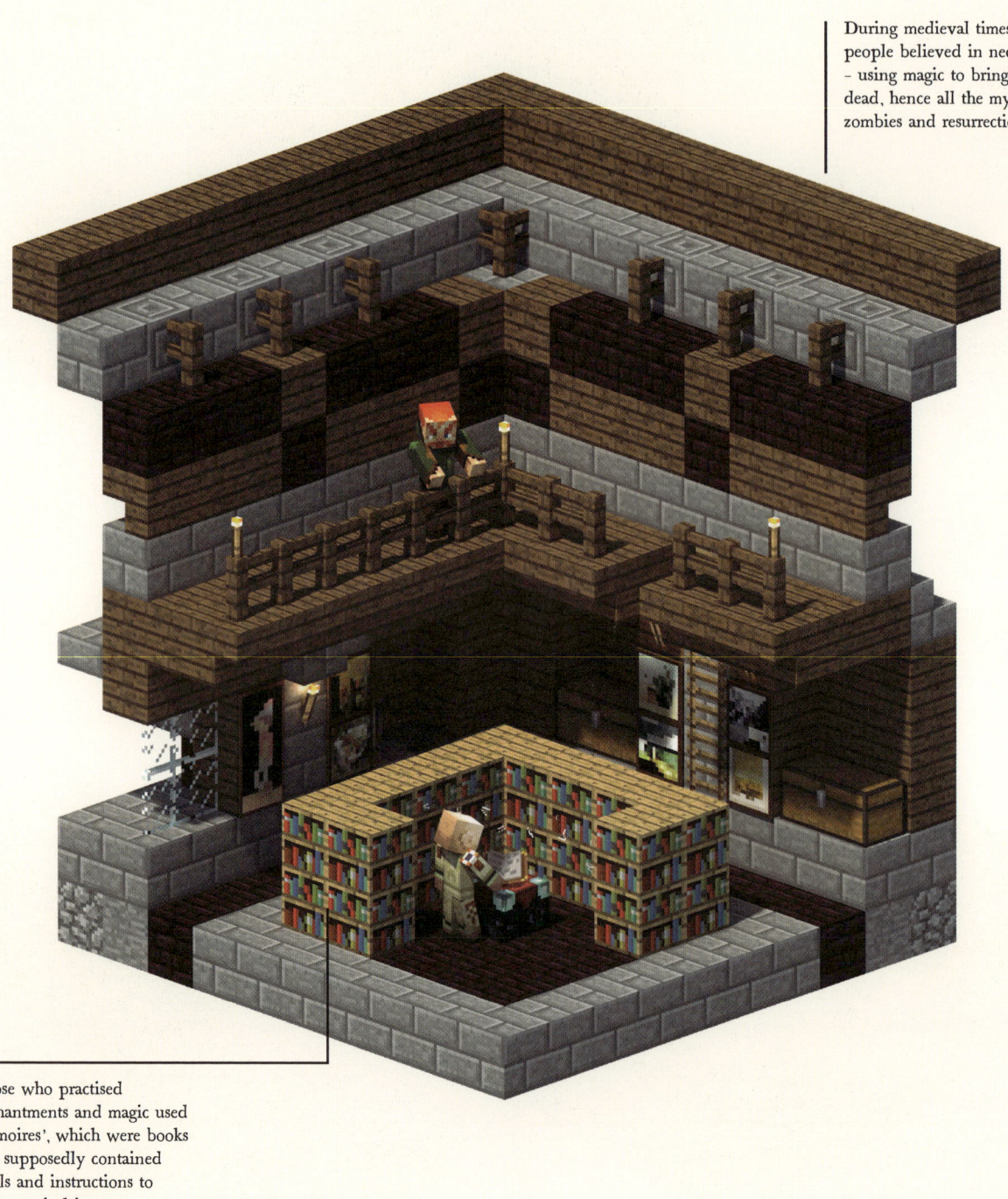

During medieval times lots of people believed in necromancy – using magic to bring back the dead, hence all the myths of zombies and resurrection.

Those who practised enchantments and magic used 'grimoires', which were books that supposedly contained spells and instructions to make magical items.

16

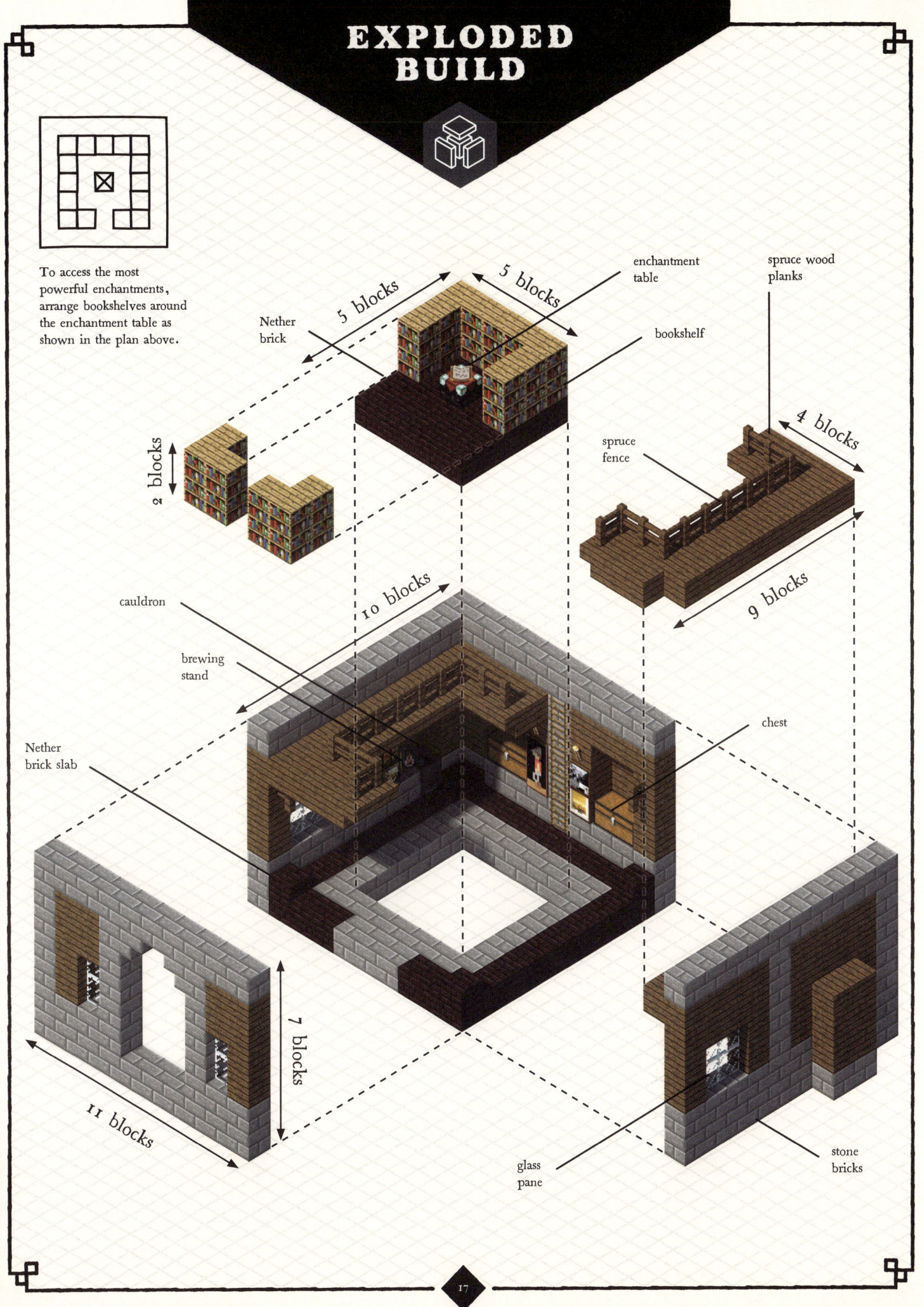

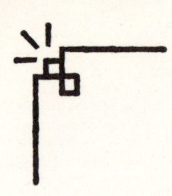

DUGEON

🕐 1 HOUR ① ② ③ ④ EASY

When the invasion of your castle has failed and your enemies have surrendered, you'll need to imprison them somewhere to teach them a lesson. A secret, secure dungeon built underneath the castle keep will detain unlucky attackers behind blocks and bars to stop them causing any more trouble.

The dungeons would have been split into individual cells, where as many as ten prisoners would be kept at once.

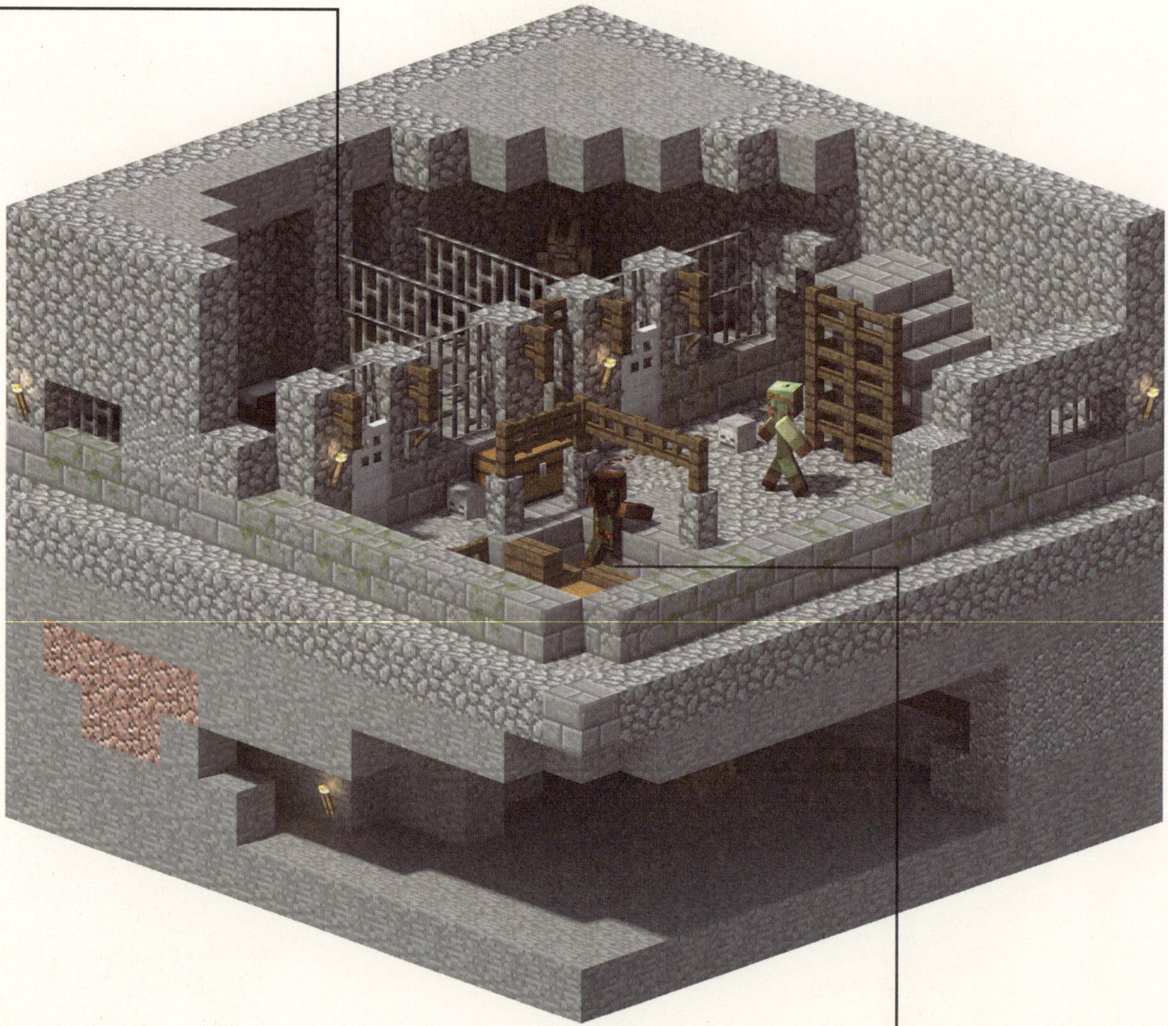

Guardsmen were stationed in dungeons to keep watch over prisoners and ferry them to and from trials.

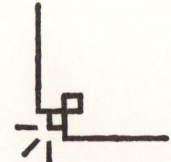
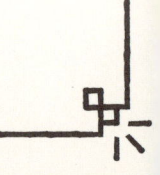

EXPLODED BUILD

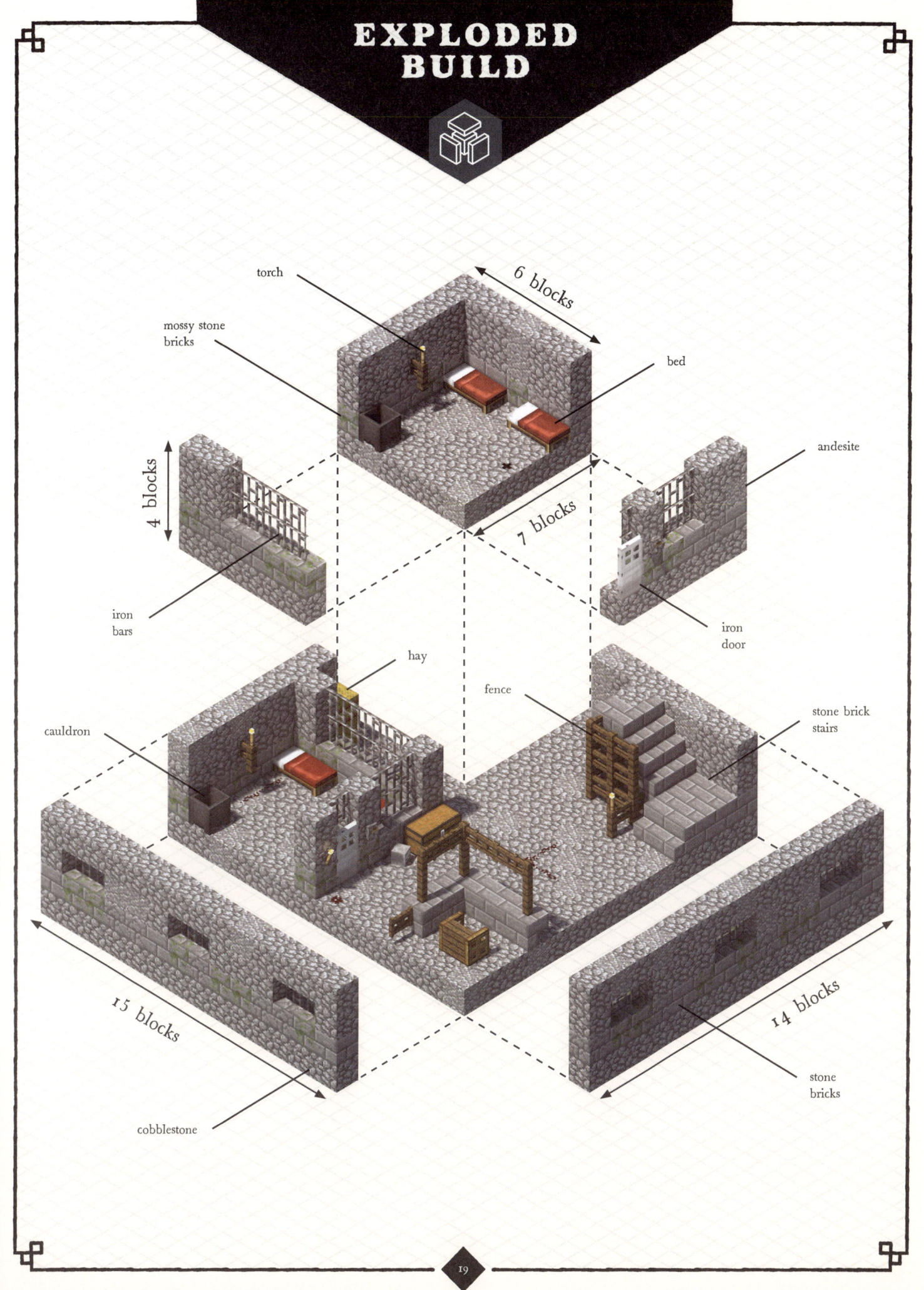

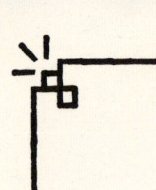

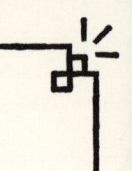

VILLAGE HOUSE

⏱ **1 HOUR**   ① ② ③ ④   **BEGINNER**

A medieval kingdom needs loyal subjects to rule over and they need somewhere to live too. Build lots of these basic houses to create somewhere for your villagers to live, thrive and hide from hostile mobs at night. Use simple blocks like wood and cobblestone to recreate the simple style of buildings that were around in medieval times.

Instead of glass windows, poorer families would have 'fenestral' windows – lattice frames covered in treated fabric.

Most houses would be built on stone foundations so that the wooden frame wouldn't rot and fall apart.

20

EXPLODED BUILD

Build Tip

The roof of the house hangs over the walls. To make this, add an extra block on front of the wall and place the stairs on top, then destroy the block.

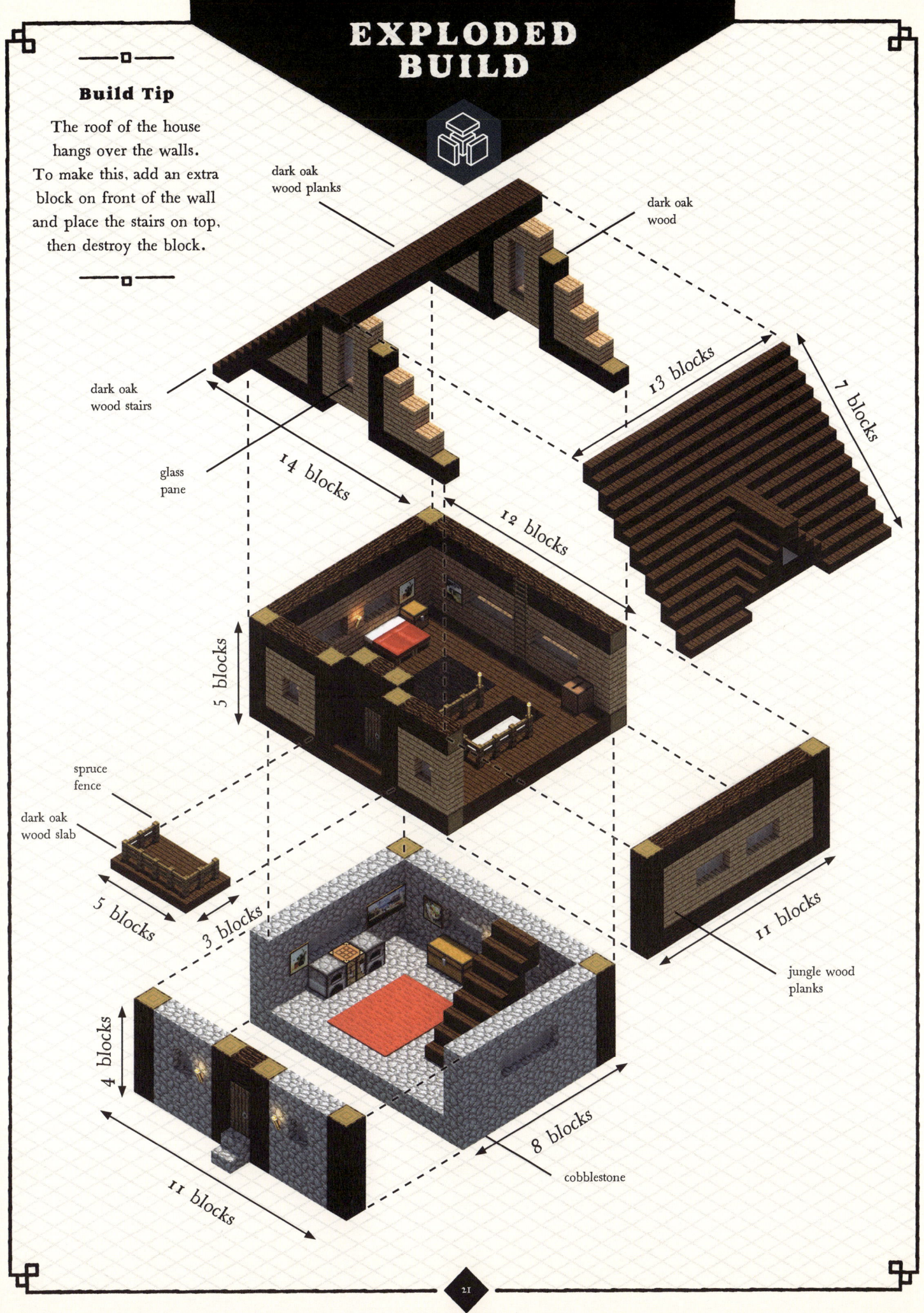

MARKET SQUARE

🕐 1 HOUR ① ② ③ ④ BEGINNER

The market square is the hub of commerce and activity in your medieval kingdom. Everything you could possibly need for your kingdom can be found at one of the stalls in the square. Townspeople will be trading everything from weapons and potions to crops like pumpkins and potatoes.

Traders would have specialised in selling a single type of item. Grocers would sell food, blacksmiths offered weapons and metalwork, whilst farmers would trade in livestock.

Markets were the heart of any town. In fact, the very definition of a town, as opposed to a village, used to be that it had a market.